Lorelei and the White Mare

PRAISE FOR *STORYSHARES*

"One of the brightest innovators and game-changers in the education industry."
– Forbes

"Your success in applying research-validated practices to promote literacy serves as a valuable model for other organizations seeking to create evidence-based literacy programs."
- Library of Congress

"We need powerful social and educational innovation, and Storyshares is breaking new ground. The organization addresses critical problems facing our students and teachers. I am excited about the strategies it brings to the collective work of making sure every student has an equal chance in life."
– Teach For America

"Around the world, this is one of the up-and-coming trailblazers changing the landscape of literacy and education."
- International Literacy Association

"It's the perfect idea. There's really nothing like this. I mean wow, this will be a wonderful experience for young people."   - Andrea Davis Pinkney, Executive Director, Scholastic

"Reading for meaning opens opportunities for a lifetime of learning. Providing emerging readers with engaging texts that are designed to offer both challenges and support for each individual will improve their lives for years to come. Storyshares is a wonderful start."
- David Rose, Co-founder of CAST & UDL

Lorelei and the White Mare

Jacqueline Kolosov

STORYSHARES

Story Share, Inc.
New York. Boston. Philadelphia

Copyright © 2022 by Jacqueline Kolosov

All rights reserved.

Published in the United States by Story Share, Inc.

The characters and events in this book are fictitious. Any similarity to real persons, living or dead, is entirely coincidental.

Storyshares
Story Share, Inc.
24 N. Bryn Mawr Avenue #340
Bryn Mawr, PA 19010-3304
www.storyshares.org

Inspiring reading with a new kind of book.

Interest Level: High School
Grade Level Equivalent: 4.5

9781973523260

Book design by Storyshares

Printed in the United States of America

Storyshares Presents

1

So many things in life, Lorelei has learned, are unreliable. The suddenness of change scares her because she can't predict it. It makes her feel like a dandelion caught up by wind. Who can say where her seeds will fall? Where will she land? Will she land?

These fears began a year ago. It was late October, and the leaves were beginning to change color.

Her mother decided to run out for some yeast and flour. She was a night owl, and she loved to bake.

That chilly, October evening, she decided to make bread. She wanted to fill the house with the smells of cinnamon and flour and butter, she said.

"I'll be back in twenty minutes," she told Lorelei, just before driving off. "And I'm counting on you to help."

Lorelei loved baking with her mother. When her mother baked, she slowed down. They talked and shared secrets. Her mother would knead the dough and tell Lorelei about her childhood in Germany. Lorelei's grandfather used to carve things from wood: a house, a child, a miniature tree. He'd even carved the legendary mermaid for whom Lorelei had been named.

These were the stories Lorelei looked forward to that evening, last October, as her mother drove off into the fading light. Meanwhile, Lorelei sat at the kitchen table and sketched the sky. She watched it turn from deep pink to violet. Drawing was something else that she and her mother loved.

Who could have predicted that a car would run the red light on the street just beyond the supermarket?

The car hit the driver's side of her mother's car. By the time the ambulance arrived, Lorelei's mother was in a coma. She died in the admitting area at Covenant

Hospital. Lorelei and her father arrived a few minutes later.

"We're too late," her father said.

The two of them stood side by side before the stretcher. Lorelei's mother's face was a pasty white. Like flour.

Lorelei said nothing.

The weather in West Texas where Lorelei lives is always changing. It is the one thing she can count on. Lorelei knows this sounds strange. But the changing weather patterns are facts. They're predictable.

In West Texas, the weather can be sunny and seventy degrees in the morning. By nightfall, the temperature can drop to thirty or below. Sometimes the wind blows so fiercely it feels like needles against the skin.

Because Lorelei knows these things are possible, she accepts them. She prepares for them, and they don't scare her.

Being prepared means taking an extra sweater or a jacket along when she leaves for school, or the stable ten miles across town.

Lorelei started working at the stable last month. Since then, she has accumulated a locker full of t-shirts, sweaters, socks, and long-sleeved flannel shirts. She can add more layers as she needs them. Or she can take them off.

She even has two different kinds of boots. She has a pair of rubber boots for mucking out stalls or hosing off the ground. Then there's the sturdy leather boots she wears out in the paddocks.

Though she stopped riding when Lorelei was seven, Lorelei's mother loved horses. This is one reason why Lorelei works Saturdays and Sundays at the stable.

The need to steady herself is the other reason Lorelei took the job. Because everything is changing.

Her mother is gone.

Her father remarried Kimberly Field in June. They are expecting a baby in February. Is it only coincidence — chance? — that Kimberly owns the bakery closest to their house? Lorelei's mother sometimes bought cakes and bread there.

    Of course, her mother only went to Kimberly's bakery when she didn't have time to make her own baked goods.

    Lorelei keeps her mother's recipes in an old wooden box. When she is sad, she takes the hand-printed cards out. She studies them carefully. She traces her mother's handwriting with her fingertips.

2

The last Saturday in November is cold and damp. The windowpanes are fogged when Lorelei wakes up. She turns up the heater before she gets dressed. Outside, the rain freezes in the air. It clings to the branches of the tree outside her window. The ice-covered branches shimmer in the early light. Lorelei would like to sketch the branches. But she must leave for the stable.

At seven o'clock, her father and Kimberly are still sleeping. But Lorelei is on her way to the stable. The temperature hovers around thirty. But at least the freezing rain has stopped.

By the time Lorelei pulls into the stable's gravel driveway, it's almost seven-thirty. A few horses nicker in the distance. The light is an opaque white.

The sun won't come out today.

Lorelei doesn't mind gray days. What she dislikes, intensely, is high wind. High wind bites her skin. High wind seeps deep into her bones.

It's quiet now. But by noon, the radio forecaster said, the winds will gust up to thirty miles an hour. By two o'clock, the winds will gust up to forty miles an hour.

As soon as Lorelei steps out of the car, the old border collie, Woody, comes to greet her. He is black and white and smells like the winter that lies ahead. She pats his cold head and fishes a dog treat from her jeans pocket.

Woody wags his tail and follows her towards the stable.

At least a dozen of the horses at Miriam Parson's stable live outside year round. Miriam says the horses don't mind the rain and snow. Lorelei isn't so sure.

Sure, horses in the wild can seek the shelter of trees. But in West Texas, there are few trees. The paddocks at the stable are made up of weedy grass. Some of the paddocks contain only dirt. Miriam compensates for this by filling the dirt-caked paddocks with a big bale of hay. She makes up for the lack of trees with a tin-roofed shelter.

But on the second Sunday that Lorelei worked there, heavy rains drenched the paddocks. The dirt turned instantly to mud. One of the old lesson horses, a kind Arabian named Moses, slipped in the mud and broke his left foreleg. He lay there, quiet, still, until someone found him.

That same night, the veterinarian drove out to the stable to put him down.

3

Cleaning the horses' stalls is repetitive. Lorelei likes that. It is another thing that she can count on. Besides, the back and forth of raking soothes Lorelei. So does the smell of the cedar chips that she uses to line the horses' stalls. Every morning she fills the wheelbarrow with them. She replenishes the horses' stalls and cleans out the manure. This makes her feel happy. She is doing something productive. She is making the lives of the horses better.

Even on a cold morning like this one, the stable smells of cedar, hay, alfalfa, manure, and horse. These smells comfort Lorelei. They resemble a flannel blanket or a very soft, very warm hat on a cold day. Sometimes the smells at the barn even remind Lorelei of her mother's baking — at least in the comfort sense.

But only sometimes. The horses look at Lorelei as she enters the smaller of the two barns. This barn has been painted a dusky pink. Lorelei drew a picture of it and hung it on her bedroom wall. As she enters, Woody follows her.

The old gelding, Noah, occupies the stall closest to the door. He whinnies impatiently.

"Just a minute. I'm coming," Lorelei says.

More horses begin to whinny. Their voices pierce the cold air.

Lorelei begins to laugh. She likes the voices of the horses. The sounds are welcoming, familiar.

She will feed and water the horses inside the two stables first. By the time she's done, it will be nearly nine o'clock. The air will still be cold, but it'll be better by the time she goes out to feed the horses in the paddock. Hopefully, the wind will not be blowing yet.

Most likely, the water in the paddocks will have frozen during the night. Lorelei will need to crack the surface with a steel pick.

Most of the stalls have small windows that Lorelei opens in order to fill the feed bins with grain. And over each bin there is a slot for hay. Only Smoke's stall doesn't have a window. Instead, Lorelei must pull open the heavy door, step inside, and fill Smoke's bin.

"Don't get too close," she tells Woody.

Smoke, a fiery old Arabian, once kicked Woody. Lorelei doesn't know if Woody remembers this. But she doesn't want to take a chance.

After feeding and watering all sixteen horses in the small pink barn, Lorelei pulls the heavy door closed. This will seal in the warmth.

Outside, the wind is stirring. She zips her parka up all the way. She tugs her hat over her ears. Then she walks across the treeless property to the big yellow barn. Here she will repeat the process all over again.

Unless a squirrel or a mouse seizes his attention, Woody will accompany her. Some days, he stays by

Lorelei's side from early morning until dusk when she leaves.

4

The chestnut-colored Lady is Lorelei's favorite horse in the big barn. A long white streak runs the length of Lady's nose. Lady is a sturdy quarter horse. She stands fifteen hands high, and she's given birth to two foals during the last five years.

"What happened to the babies?" Lorelei asked Miriam Parsons once.

"Sold," Miriam said matter-of-factly.

"Doesn't Lady miss them?" Lorelei asked.

"No, of course not," Miriam said.

Lorelei didn't say anything to Miriam, but she believes that Lady does miss her babies. How could she not?

And the fact that Lady has lost someone she loves — two someones — makes her dear to Lorelei.

Lorelei always gives Lady extra hay. This morning she fishes for a carrot deep in her backpack. Even though it's cold, Lorelei removes her glove when she feeds Lady the carrot. She loves the feel of Lady's whiskery lips on her skin.

"It's bitter out there today," Lorelei tells the horse as she eats. "I guess I have to bring you outside anyway. But I think you'd be happier here where it's warm."

Lady just nickers.

From the other stalls, horses begin to whinny. They, too, want their breakfasts. Their impatient voices tell Lorelei that she's taking too long.

"I'm coming, I'm coming," she tells them, as she closes the door to Lady's stall. At her feet, Woody wags his long brush of a tail. "Good boy," she tells him.

She continues her work, humming a little as she moves from stall to stall.

Turns out, the radio forecaster got the weather wrong. Yes, the wind picks up as the morning wears on. By nine fifteen, Lorelei has turned the last of thirty-three horses into one of the six paddocks on the property. The wind is blowing. But it's nowhere near as bad as the forecaster predicted.

Lorelei takes Lady out last. She releases her into a paddock with patches of weedy grass. "Have a good day, girl," she says, rubbing the mare's nose.

Turning back towards the barn, Lorelei thinks about the hot chocolate she will pour from her thermos. She will drop in a few marshmallows from the bag she keeps in her locker. Before she gets to work cleaning the stalls, she will cradle the cup in her hands. She will dip the bread she has brought into the hot drink.

She baked the bread herself from her mother's recipe. Her mother wrote the recipe out in red ink. It's an old recipe, and the writing is beginning to fade. The last time Lorelei used the recipe, she traced over her mother's letters carefully. In order to preserve them, she makes sure to keep the recipe cards out of direct sunlight.

5

Sunday morning is milder than the morning before. Lorelei wakes to cool air, but the temperature is closer to forty degrees. Driving to the barn, she watches the sun rise. She feels happier than she has in a long time. And she's eager to see the horses. She is eager to hear them nicker and whinny when she enters the barn. She will fill their bins with grain and hay. And they, too, will be happy.

Lady couldn't keep her foals. But there is a little female filly at the barn. Her name is Copper Penny. She was born in the middle of May, just before the weather turned too warm.

"If I can find the time, I'm going to begin weaning her before Christmas," Marion tells Lorelei that morning. Lorelei is standing outside the enclosed pen that Copper Penny shares with her mother, Daisy, a paint horse.

Like her mother, Copper Penny's white fur is patched with rust-colored swatches. Her mane stands on end like a mohawk. She is a playful creature. Lorelei loves watching Copper Penny frolic in the pen. This morning, Copper kicks up her strong, thin legs.

"Yes," Marion says. "By Christmas, she'll be ready to be weaned."

Lorelei understands that this is necessary. Still, when she thinks about the separation of mother and filly, she feels a little sad. She knows this is partly due to her own mother's absence. But she also remembers the comfort she felt, as a small child, being around her mother.

Surely, she thinks, a young horse feels that comfort, too. Weaning will mean separation, a loss of that comfort.

Still, there is nothing she can do. Marion knows horses, having been around them all her life. The stable, now Marion's, once belonged to her grandmother. Marion's grandmother raised and cared for her just as she raised and cared for the horses. What happened to Marion's mother, Lorelei doesn't know.

Lorelei's work that Sunday moves quickly. She hums a little as she goes. It's partly the weather. By ten o'clock, the sun has broken through the clouds, and temperature is warming up.

"A new horse is going to arrive later today," Marion says.

Marion follows Lorelei out to the paddocks. Lorelei is pushing a wheelbarrow overflowing with flakes — brick-like wedges — of hay.

The horses know that food is coming. They approach the fence. They nicker.

"Where are you going to put him?" Lorelei asks.

"Her," Marion corrects. "The horse is a mare."

Lorelei nods. She is focused on distributing the flakes of hay to the horses. "Where are you going to put her?"

"In Timothy's old stall," Marion says. "After you finish out here, I'd like you to clean it out."

Lorelei's heart skips a beat.

Timothy died a few days after Lorelei started working at the barn. He lived to the ripe old age of thirty. "A rare thing for a horse," Marion said.

Twelve years ago, Lorelei's family moved to West Texas from Chicago. In the spring of that year, Lorelei's mother began riding again. "To get used to the country out here," she said. "To make it feel more familiar."

Lorelei's father understood, for Lorelei's mother had first learned to ride when she was a girl in Germany.

When she began coming to the stable, Lorelei's mother would ride Timothy.

Timothy had a beautiful, pale gold coat and mane back then.

Sometime after Lorelei started school, her mother stopped riding. She said it was time to start saving for Lorelei's education. She said riding was too expensive.

Even so, Lorelei's mother sometimes came out to the barn to see Timothy. She used to bring him carrots and the tart Granny Smith apples he loved. Sometimes, Lorelei came with her.

Lorelei knows that Timothy's stall couldn't stay empty forever. She just can't imagine another horse inhabiting it.

"Come find me in the big barn when you're done out here," Marion tells her. "The stall will have to be done in a hurry."

Lorelei and the White Mare

6

"Of course," Lorelei says. She listens to Marion's footsteps on the gravel path. They grow softer as she moves further away.

Lorelei spends the next two hours cleaning Timothy's former stall. She wears latex gloves to scrub the walls with a mixture of bleach and hot water.

Marion helps as much as she can in between lessons. But Sunday afternoon is a busy day for children learning to ride. So Lorelei has to do most of the work alone.

Lorelei wipes down the walls with an old towel to speed the drying process. Next, she fills a wheelbarrow with cedar shavings and begins to fill the stall.

"No, no," Marion calls out.

Lorelei startles. "What's wrong?"

"The owner requested straw for the bedding."

Lorelei stops in her tracks. "Straw? But isn't that more expensive?"

"Yes," Marion says. "Sorry, I should have told you sooner."

* * *

The horse that steps out of the trailer at three o'clock is like no other horse that Lorelei has seen. She is like a horse out of a fairy tale. She is a snowy white with an equally white mane and tail.

It's not just that the horse is beautiful. There's something mysterious about her, too. A quality that reminds Lorelei of starlight and prayer.

"What's her name?" Lorelei asks as Marion leads the horse to her new stall.

"Artemis," Marion says.

"Isn't that a mythological name?" Lorelei asks, remembering hearing a name like that in English class when they studied myths.

"Artemis is the goddess of the moon, I think," Marion says.

"She protects women and children," another voice calls out.

Lorelei spins around. Marcus is smiling at her.

"Marcus," she says. "I didn't see you there."

"And I certainly didn't think you knew much about Greek goddesses, Marcus," Marion says.

"I'm a man of many surprises," Marcus tells her. "By the way, Artemis is a Roman name. The Greek equivalent is Diana."

The word beats through Lorelei's brain. How many months now since she's heard that name? She reaches out to steady herself. But it's too late. The next thing she knows, she's falling into a bed of very soft straw.

7

"My mother's name was Diana," Lorelei tells Marcus later. They are sitting on a rough wooden bench facing the riding arena.

"Oh, yes," Marcus says.

Lorelei bites her lip. She's afraid she might cry. "You know? You knew her name?"

"Yes. I heard about your mother's accident," Marcus says.

Of course. It was all over the papers. Lorelei feels her eyes fill with tears. She wipes them away, bites her lip to keep from crying.

"I'm sorry," he says, and covers her hand with his own.

"I miss her," Lorelei whispers.

Marcus nods. "I can't even imagine how much," he says. "My mom died when I was four."

Lorelei looks up at him. "Really?"

He nods. "She got cancer when I was three. Sometime during the winter she went into the hospital and never came home. The worst part is I hardly remember her."

The memories that Lorelei has of her mother make her feel windy inside. Lonely.

But they can also be a source of comfort and connection. She cannot imagine her life without those memories now.

"I'm sorry for you, too," she says.

He nods. "Yes, well, it was a long, long time ago."

They sit in silence. On the far end of the arena, some of the horses are munching on hay. Others shuffle around in their stalls. The sounds are familiar, pleasant.

"What do you say we get dinner after you finish up here?" Marcus asks.

Lorelei just gazes into his blue eyes. She is thinking about how handsome Marcus is. But she is also thinking about the white mare. And she is thinking about her mother.

"Dinner?" Marcus asks again.

"I still have so much to do," Lorelei says.

"I can help you finish up. Come on," he says. "There's a new Thai restaurant that's opened up. I'd like to try it."

Lorelei can't remember the last time she ate at a restaurant.

"Well?" Marcus presses.

"All right," Lorelei says. "Why not?"

It's not until they climb into Marcus's pickup that Lorelei remembers her car.

"Shouldn't I follow you?" she asks.

"Why don't I bring you back out here after supper?"

Lorelei looks puzzled. "But that doesn't make sense."

"Maybe not, but I'd like some company," he says. "It's a long way into town."

"All right, then," Lorelei answers. She doesn't tell him that she has grown used to the silence. She doesn't say that she likes it.

The Thai restaurant is not what Lorelei expected. She expected Formica table tops and aluminum chairs with plastic flowers in a vase or a single, fading rose.

But this place has special, soft lights. The walls have been painted a dusky chocolate. The tables and chairs are made of dark wood. Bunches of yellow daisies fill the vases on every table. Candles glow.

"Look at this," Lorelei hears herself say, pointing to the bronze goddess near the door.

"What, you don't like it?" Marcus asks. They are standing in the entryway and waiting to be seated.

"Of course I like it," Lorelei says. "It's just that the whole place is fancier than I expected."

Marcus laughs. "My treat," he says.

8

They order a coconut soup with lemongrass to start. Actually, Marcus orders it. "Let's share," he says. "That way we can try different dishes."

Lorelei nods. She doesn't know what lemongrass is. She wonders if the horses would eat it.

"What looks good to you?" he asks.

She grins, sheepish, her cheeks reddening. "The egg rolls," she says.

"And I like anything with noodles. But no meat," she adds.

"No problem," Marcus says. "Let's order the vegetable egg rolls and the sesame noodles."

The waitress arrives. "Ready to order?"

Lorelei would have repeated the numbers of each entree. But Marcus can actually pronounce the names.

"How did you learn to do that?" she says.

He shrugs. "I lived in San Francisco for a while with my dad," he says. "He loves Thai food."

Lorelei nods. She never thought about where Marcus came from, where he had lived before. She just assumed he'd always been in Texas.

"How about you?" Marcus asks.

Having taken their order, the waitress lights the candle on their table.

She bows before leaving.

Lorelei looks confused. "How about me what?"

"Have you always lived in Texas?"

Lorelei shakes her head. "I was born in Chicago. We moved to Lubbock when I was four."

"I've always wanted to visit Chicago," Marcus says.

"It's a great city," Lorelei tells him.

"Do you still go back?"

"Not so much anymore," Lorelei says, reminded of the trips she used to take with her mom. They'd spend hours at the Art Institute or gazing at the shop windows on Michigan Avenue. And always, there were their splurges at Pizzeria Uno. "My uncle's still there, but since my mom died, it's not the same."

Marcus nods, and Lorelei meets his gaze. His eyes really are incredibly blue. For a moment, she wonders why he has asked her here. Marcus is at least twenty-two. His dark brown hair is thick and wavy, and he has high cheekbones, thanks to his Cherokee ancestry. He's very popular at the barn.

And here Lorelei is, a sixteen-year-old stall mucker who doesn't smile or talk much anymore. She's wearing dirty jeans and muddy boots. There is mud on her chin. And most embarrassing of all, today she actually fainted.

The egg rolls arrive first, and then the coconut soup with lemongrass.

Marcus spoons some into Lorelei's bowl, then his own.

"Do you like it?" he asks.

"Yes." She is surprised at how good it is.

They talk about the stable. He tells her about his experience as a riding instructor. "I went to college for two years. I thought I'd study math."

"But you left?" Lorelei says.

"Yeah." He grows quiet, lays down his spoon.

"Why?"

"I was unhappy," he says. "College was my father's dream, not my own."

"Was he very disappointed? Your father, I mean?" Lorelei asks.

"At first," Marcus says. "He never went to college himself. He works construction. He's got his own business now, and he's very successful. Still, he wanted me to have that degree. Fortunately, when he saw how happy I am at the stable, teaching..."

"He came around?" Lorelei says.

"Exactly," Marcus answers, and smiles. "He came around."

"Did your father get married again?" Lorelei asks. She is thinking about her own father and Kimberly and the baby they will have in February. At night, they curl up before the TV. They hold hands and share popcorn from a big bowl.

"No," Marcus says. "He never did."

She doesn't need to tell Marcus that her father remarried. She's seen him in Kimberly's bakery.

"My dad and Kimberly are having a baby in February," she says.

"Are you happy about that?"

"Honestly, I don't know," Lorelei says. "It's all just so soon, you know? I mean, my mom's been gone just over a year, and here he is, starting over again. I'm not ready..."

He puts an arm around her shoulder. "Sometimes," he says, "we don't get a choice."

* * *

It's almost eight o'clock by the time Marcus drops Lorelei off at the barn. She wonders if this is a date. She wonders if Marcus will kiss her.

But they just shake hands. "I guess I'll see you on Saturday," he says.

"Yes, Saturday," she replies.

The moon moves in and out of the clouds. When it disappears behind the clouds, the landscape is dark. This makes it hard to see.

"Well," Marcus says. "You should get going. And so should I."

"Thank you for dinner," Lorelei says.

On the way home, she thinks about Marcus. He was so kind, a really good listener. She doesn't know many people like that.

After a while, her thoughts turn to the white mare inside the barn. Is she frightened? Lorelei wonders. Does she trust her new surroundings?

The mare's name is Artemis, but she is also Diana.

"Mom," Lorelei says aloud. "I wish you were here."

9

There's nothing fancy about the house that Lorelei grew up in. It's a small, white house with aluminum siding and a faux-shingle roof. Why would anyone want fake shingles? (Lorelei used to ask her father. His answers never satisfied her.)

Last summer, Lorelei's mother painted the shutters and the doorway green. "To make the house more cheerful," she said.

The best part about the house is its location. It's on the outskirts of town. There are actually live oak trees and a few maples behind the house. The trees belong to Homer Watkins. He teaches at the university. Mr. Watkins specializes in birds.

"Birds like trees," Mr. Watkins told Lorelei once. "That's why I planted them."

Mr. Watkins is nearly sixty. He has lived in his house for forty years. The trees have grown tall.

It's after dark when Lorelei arrives home that evening. The light in the kitchen window is on. This is a sign that her father and Kimberly are making dinner. Maybe they have already eaten.

They did this last Saturday when Lorelei came home at eight o'clock. She didn't tell them that she stayed at the stable to talk to Marcus Willems, one of the riding instructors. Marcus has clear blue eyes that remind Lorelei of the sky on a sunny day. He speaks softly. Lorelei can see that he is gentle with people and horses.

"Good, you're home," her father calls when she steps inside. "We were just about to eat."

Kimberly is right behind him. "I'm craving fried chicken tonight."

Lorelei doesn't remind Kimberly that she doesn't like fried chicken. She doesn't remind Kimberly that she doesn't eat meat at all these days.

Kimberly, Lorelei believes, would not remember anyway.

Tucked away in her cat bed near the stove is Misha. "Hi there, old girl," Lorelei says, bending to stroke Misha's silky, black fur. The cat purrs in response. She closes her big, yellow eyes. When she opens them, the yellows hold sharp diamonds.

Misha is Kimberly's cat. Maybe this should be a strike against her, at least in Lorelei's mind. But the cat is so friendly. She twines around Lorelei's legs. Sometimes she even curls up on Lorelei's pillow.

In the six months that her father and Kimberly have been married, Lorelei has grown fond of this cat.

Kimberly brings the chicken to the table. Lorelei's father sets down a leafy salad with slices of avocado and mandarin oranges. Her father and Kimberly will each have a glass of white wine.

"Just a small glass won't hurt the baby," Kimberly says.

Kimberly loves wine, and sometimes Lorelei thinks Kimberly drinks too much. But her father never comments on his new wife's passion for wine.

Lorelei brings cheese and more of the bread she baked to the table. Slicing it, she is reminded of the thick piece she shared with Woody at lunch time. She also gave him some hot chocolate. The foam coated his whiskers.

As her father and Kimberly talk, Lorelei's thoughts turn to Marcus. She looked around for him that day, but he never showed up. Usually he teaches lessons on the weekends. Later, Marion told Lorelei that Marcus had driven to Amarillo to look at a horse for one of his students.

Before sitting down, Lorelei pours herself a tall glass of milk. She fills a saucer for Misha.

"That cat is getting spoiled, living with you," Kimberly says.

"She's not spoiled," Lorelei replies. "She's just well taken care of."

Her father asks her a little bit about the work at the stable. He wants to know about the weather and the horses. She answers him, but she speaks mostly in single syllables.

It's her father and Kimberly who do most of the talking. The baby isn't due for another three months. Still, they are already deep into planning the nursery.

Kimberly hopes the baby will be a little girl. "I've always wanted a daughter," she says.

Lorelei's father looks down at his plate when Kimberly says this. He doesn't speak for a long time.

After helping with the dishes, Lorelei climbs the narrow staircase to her room. It's only nine o'clock, but she will have to wake up at six thirty. She is due at the stable again on Sunday morning. Working all day in the cold makes her especially tired.

Lorelei's best friend Margaret doesn't understand why Lorelei works such long hours. "You have to go to bed so early. Your weekends are shot."

Lorelei doesn't see it that way. She likes the exhaustion. She likes the heaviness of her arms and legs as she climbs into bed. She likes the fact that it's hard to keep her eyes open past ten.

"Being tired keeps me from thinking," Lorelei told Margaret once.

Margaret didn't say anything, but Lorelei believed she understood.

After all, Margaret and Lorelei have known each other since first grade. Margaret held Lorelei's hand at the funeral. She came to see her every day, even on the days when Lorelei couldn't speak much.

Tonight Lorelei picks up a book to read. It's a novel required for school. Lorelei likes disappearing into stories, entering other people's lives. But tonight she can't keep her eyes open. It's not quite nine thirty when she switches off the light.

When Lorelei feels Misha kneading the pillow with her paws, she smiles and reaches a sleepy hand out. She strokes the cat.

"Good night," she whispers. She dozes off listening to Misha's gravelly purr.

10

Lorelei is a junior at Lubbock High School. Buddy Holly, the musician, once went to school there. The hallway has a plaque about that on the wall. There is another plaque in the music studio.

Lorelei used to play the piano, but these days her favorite classes are Art and English. She dislikes Algebra and finds Home Economics to be a waste of time.

After all, Lorelei's mother taught her more about making a home than any class could. Lorelei's bread is far better than the teacher's.

At two o'clock every day, Lorelei has gym class. This semester, she has signed up for swimming. She could not have expected how much she would enjoy it.

In the steamy locker room, she changes into her red and white bathing suit. She showers off before entering the pool.

The tiles feel cool beneath her feet. The air smells of chlorine. The water in the natatorium — a fancy word for swimming pool — is aquamarine.

At first, Lorelei used the ladder to ease her way into the water. At first, she was reluctant to get her hair wet, and she hated the feel of water in her eyes.

Now, she likes to plunge head-first into the deep end. This is an accomplishment, something she could not do one month ago.

After swimming the required number of laps, she lies on her back. She closes her eyes. And for a little while, the world disappears.

She forgets about her father and Kimberly and the baby that they are expecting.

She doesn't think about the fact that her mother is gone.

She just lets the water lap over her. She listens to its rhythm. She feels at peace.

After showering, Lorelei gets dressed in the locker room. She feels clean and new. It's almost as if she's starting her day all over again.

Best of all, after swimming, the school day is over. She meets Margaret outside the locker room. Margaret has signed up for dance this semester. She dislikes chlorine and gets cold easily.

"Besides," she says, "chlorine would ruin my hair."

"Do you have time for a coffee?" Margaret asks on Friday.

Unlike the auburn-haired Lorelei, who freckles in sun, Margaret is very blonde and pale. She likes to wear neutral colors like beige and dark brown and olive green.

Margaret is tall and thin. Her neck is very long. For a year, she considered going to New York to become a model. But her father said, "You are too smart to become a walking advertisement for clothes."

Margaret didn't protest. "New York's a polluted city, anyway," she told Lorelei.

These days, Margaret plans to go to college and study engineering like her parents. Or else, she says, she'll become a high school teacher. She'd like to teach math, the one subject that Lorelei has never been any good at. This is probably the biggest difference between them. Whereas Lorelei loves art and literature, Margaret gravitates towards math and problem-solving.

At the Divine Grind Coffee Shop, Margaret orders a "grande" cappuccino with extra cocoa sprinkles. Lorelei prefers English Breakfast tea with milk. They share a cinnamon scone.

As they eat, Lorelei thinks about her mother's scone recipe. Her mother always used dried cherries in her scones. She also thinks about her dinner with Marcus. And she thinks about the white mare, Artemis. Both of them, she will see tomorrow.

"Earth to Lorelei," Margaret says, tapping her fingers against the tabletop.

"Sorry," Lorelei says. "I guess I'm tired."

Margaret raises an eyebrow. "Preoccupied is more like it. What gives?"

"Nothing," Lorelei says. She is not ready to talk about the mare or Marcus, not even with Margaret.

"How's Kimberly?" Margaret asks now.

Since Lorelei's father married Kimberly, Margaret has become suspicious of her. "The woman's after something," is what Margaret said when Lorelei's father married her.

"But what could she be after?" Lorelei wanted to ask. "It's not like my father is rich or handsome. It's not like our house is anything special. And he has me — a teenage daughter. What exactly is Kimberly getting out of this?"

But she never asked the question. She never asked, because deep down she knows that Kimberly has won a prize in marrying her father. He is a kind man, and he is generous. He brings Kimberly flowers just as he once brought Lorelei's mother flowers. He always unloads the dishwasher.

And he does laundry, not just his own, but everyone's. This was one of the things that Lorelei's mother loved about him. "A man who will wash and fold your socks and underwear is a treasure, my dear," she used to tell Lorelei. "Remember that."

And when he married Kimberly, he was sad and lonely. Now, he is neither. Now, he has a new wife, and in a few months there will be a new baby.

Maybe Lorelei should be happy that her father found Kimberly. She would like to be, except that their love seems to leave no place for her.

Kimberly is ordering baby furniture for the nursery. She is looking at fabric swatches, considering colors.

Meanwhile, Lorelei's room could use a fresh coat of paint. Her quilt is becoming ratty. But no one notices these things. No one except Lorelei.

"You're going to come over after you work at the stable tomorrow, right?" Margaret asks just before leaving.

"Yes, of course."

"Good." Margaret seems to relax. "See you tomorrow then."

They hug goodbye.

11

On Saturday morning, Lorelei wakes before the alarm. She feels full of energy and anticipation.

Before leaving, she fixes breakfast: gingerbread and hot tea with steamed milk. After packing her lunch and putting on her jacket, she drives off. No traffic on the county roads this morning, and no bad weather means that she arrives at the stable earlier than usual.

As always, Woody is there to greet her. As always, she gives him a dog treat from her pocket. "Hi there, friend," she says, rubbing him under his chin. This morning, there are burrs trapped in his fur. "We'll have to cut them out," she tells him.

She steps out of her car and her thoughts turn to the white mare, Artemis. Yet she holds back from hurrying into the big barn to see her.

Instead, she follows her routine and heads for the small barn first. As she draws near, the horses hear her footsteps on the gravel. Hungry for their breakfast, they whinny and nicker.

An hour later, Lorelei steps into the big barn. The white mare occupies a stall at the far end. Slowly, Lorelei makes her way over to her. As she fills each bin with grain, she talks to the horses. "Good morning, Mickey," she says to the heavy-set Dutch warmblood.

"Your ear is looking better today," she tells Black Bandit. Last Sunday another horse bit him.

"How are you today, lovely Lady?" she says. This morning, as on most mornings, Lorelei gives the pretty chestnut mare a carrot.

"And you, Dakota," she says to Marcus's big bay, "how are you?"

Dakota whinnies a cheerful reply, and she heaps the grain into his bin. Reminded of Marcus's kindness, she gives Dakota extra. When she draws near the white mare's stall, her heartbeat quickens. Stop, Lorelei tells herself. She's just a horse.

But she doesn't quite believe this to be true.

She's seized with the feeling that the white mare has been waiting for her. Lorelei fills her bin with grain. She places a flake of hay in the rack above the bin. The white mare watches Lorelei, but she does not step forward to eat. This is unusual. Most horses, Lorelei has learned, are eager for their breakfasts.

But the white mare stays quiet.

"Do you like it here?" Lorelei hears herself say.

The horse comes closer. She sniffs Lorelei's sleeve. Then she nuzzles Lorelei's hand.

Lorelei can't explain it, but it's almost as if her mother is beside her. A single tear escapes from her eye.

"My mother would have liked you," she says softly. "You share her name."

Marion and many of the other people at the stable say that horses don't understand language. They can pick up a tone of voice.

Short words like "quit" or "good girl," but nothing more.

Right now, Lorelei knows this isn't true. Right now, Lorelei believes the white mare is listening closely. She believes the white mare understands.

Lorelei has never lingered for very long in a horse's stall. Yes, she has stayed a moment to talk to Lady. She has scratched Noah behind the ears. She has checked to make sure that one or another horse's injury is healing.

But she has never lingered for more than a few minutes. How could she? There's always far too much work for her to do.

This morning is different. This morning Lorelei stays with the white mare. She hears herself telling the horse about her mother's accident. She tells the horse how lonely she feels without her mother.

But Lorelei also tells her about the hours she and her mother spent baking. She talks about her mother's paintings.

"I've kept them all," Lorelei says. "One day, when I have a child, I will frame each one. I will hang the paintings in my child's room. I will tell my child about her grandmother."

Until now, Lorelei never thought about having a child of her own. But now, she knows that she will. One day.

On the other side of the barn, the horses whinny. They want their breakfasts. They are growing impatient.

"I'd better go," Lorelei says.

The mare gazes back. Her lashes are as white as her mane and tail.

Only after Lorelei has gone does she hear the mare go to her food bin and begin to eat.

12

On Sunday afternoon, Lorelei and Marcus sit together in the sunshine and share their sandwiches. Lorelei has brought peanut butter and jelly on whole wheat bread that she baked herself. Marcus's sandwich is egg salad with sweet pickles.

In between eating, Lorelei sketches in her drawing pad. This afternoon she has sketched a tree, the old tractor, and Marcus's hand. When she has more time, she will sketch the white mare. Maybe she'll even stay on after she finishes working to do so.

"Who does Artemis belong to?" Lorelei asks after awhile.

"An older woman who just moved back to Lubbock from Albuquerque, I think. Her name is Peggy Sheffield." Marcus pronounces the name as if it should mean something to Lorelei.

"Who is she?" Lorelei asks. "What's she like?"

"Her father was one of the university's first presidents. Later, he served in Congress. He made a big donation. With the money, the university built a riding arena."

Lorelei frowns. "I didn't think the university had an arena."

"It's on the other side of the university, not far from the stadium. It's used for therapeutic riding," Marcus says.

"What's that?"

"Riding for people with disabilities and special needs. Peggy Sheffield's younger sister had Down Syndrome. Therapeutic riding saved her sister's life." Marcus's face turns thoughtful. "At least that's what Mrs. Sheffield says."

"She told you this?" Lorelei says. "You've spoken to her?"

"Just once." He takes a long swallow of Coke. "She came in on Wednesday to check on Artemis." He looks over her shoulder at her drawing of the tractor. "This is really good, you know. Have you ever thought about doing it professionally?"

She smiles. "Not really. It's just something that makes me happy."

"I get that," Marcus says. "Still, you've got talent, as my dad would say."

"You said Mrs. Sheffield's old," she says, changing the topic. "How old is old?"

"Hard to say. She's really fit," Marcus says. "But I'd guess that she's at least seventy."

Lorelei thinks about this. The oldest person who rides at the stable is Lulu Ramirez. She's in her sixties, and she mostly walks her old gray horse around the arena. Even so, Lorelei can sense the pleasure that Lulu and her horse feel in each other's company.

"Does Mrs. Sheffield still ride?" Lorelei asks.

"Not too much," Marcus says. "What's cool is that she raised Artemis herself."

"Really?" Lorelei pictures a newborn foal with unsteady legs. She is very interested now.

"Yeah. Artemis's mother was Mrs. Sheffield's favorite horse. She told me that they had twenty-seven healthy years together."

"Wow."

"That's a long life for a horse. They won several competitions, apparently."

Lorelei reaches into her backpack. She has wrapped up two butterscotch brownies. She offers one to Marcus.

"Your recipe?" he asks.

"My mother's."

He nods, thoughtful. "I have an idea."

Lorelei takes a swig of milk, looks at him. "Okay."

"Why don't I ask Mrs. Sheffield if I could walk around the arena with you on Artemis's back?"

"The last time I was on a horse it was on a carousel," Lorelei says.

Every autumn, her mother took her to the state fair. And every year until Lorelei was fourteen, she rode the horses on the carousel.

"Carousel, huh?" Marcus laughs. "That's okay," he says. "I could give you a few basic cues. Besides, I won't put a bridle on her. I'll walk her around the arena with a lead rope.

"You'd do that for me?" Lorelei says.

"Sure," Marcus says, his clear blue eyes wide, open-looking. "I mean, you did make these brownies."

"Okay, I'd like that," Lorelei tells him. "I'd like that a lot." Lorelei smiles, and her grin fills her up inside and out.

Marcus nods. "She must have been one incredible baker."

"She was beyond incredible," Lorelei says. "She was stupendous."

Walking back to the barn, Lorelei realizes that's how she feels right now.

Stupendous.

13

A few days later, Lorelei has a dream. The white mare is in the dream, but she's not alone. There's another horse beside her. The horse is just as white, and the two stand close together.

Not much happens in the dream, but Lorelei understands that the other horse is a mare, too. The other horse might be the white mare's daughter. Or perhaps the other horse is the white mare's mother.

When Lorelei wakes up, she feels as if something heavy has been lifted from her body. All day, she seems to float.

***

At school, Margaret asks her if she's in love. "It's that Marcus guy from the stable, isn't it?" she says. "He asked you out again?"

"No," Lorelei says. "And that dinner last Saturday, well, I wouldn't exactly call it a date."

"No?" Margaret raises an eyebrow. "What would you call it then?"

"A meal between coworkers," she says, trying to keep a straight face.

Margaret snorts with laughter. "Come on, Lorelei, he treated you."

Lorelei shrugs despite the butterflies in her stomach. "Yes, he did."

Margaret may be Lorelei's best friend, but she hasn't told her what Marcus said on Sunday about putting her on Artemis. It's not that she's keeping it a secret. It's just that she doesn't want to jinx it.

After all, Lorelei thinks, Ms. Sheffield might not like the idea of a stranger sitting on her horse's back.

*　*　*

Without stopping to think about it, all week Lorelei finds that she is being nicer to Kimberly. She even offers to help her paint the nursery. "Once you decide on a color, that is," Lorelei says.

"Thanks," Kimberly says. "I would like that."

Afterwards, not much changes on Kimberly's end. She doesn't ask Lorelei about her school day. She isn't especially interested in Lorelei's work at the stable.

Even so, Lorelei feels better. Sometimes, she even thinks she could be happy about the baby that's coming. After all, she always wanted a sibling.

A few years ago, Lorelei asked her mother why she and her father had never had another child. "Because you were always enough for me," Lorelei's mother had said.

Until her mother died, being an only child had made Lorelei feel special. Now, though, she wishes she had someone else. A brother or sister with whom she could share memories of her mother.

*　*　*

Monday, Tuesday, and Wednesday go by slowly. At school, Lorelei makes a clay sculpture of a horse in art class. She practices the back stroke in swimming class. She tells herself that she isn't waiting to hear back from Ms. Sheffield.

But the truth is, she feels incredible suspense.

Finally, on Thursday afternoon, Marcus calls.

"Did you talk to Mrs. Sheffield?" Lorelei asks as soon as she picks up.

"I did."

"And?" Lorelei is standing on Broadway. She cups her hand over the cell phone in order to hear. "What did she say?"

"She said to call her 'Peggy,' and she said she'd like to meet you first," Marcus tells her. "But I think she likes the idea."

"When?" Lorelei says, no longer able to contain her excitement.

"I told her that you work on Saturday. She said she would come by at lunch."

"Okay," Lorelei says, "but I'll be a muddy mess."

"So what?" Marcus says. "She knows you work at the stable."

Lorelei doesn't know what to say to this.

"It's a plan, then," Marcus says.

"Looks like it," says Lorelei. "Thank you for asking her."

"No problem," Marcus says. "Truth is, I'm looking forward to it, too."

For the rest of the day, Lorelei feels as if someone has released a cache of butterflies into her body. They flutter through her ribcage, tickle her spine. She laughs and smiles easily.

* * *

"You're awfully keyed up today, Lorelei," her father says on Friday evening. They are gathered around the dinner table, finishing their butternut squash soup.

"Keyed up" had been her mother's phrase, and Lorelei startles at the familiar words.

"I suppose I am," she says, but she doesn't give anything else away.

After talking to Marcus, she stopped by the resale shop and found a blue and yellow quilt for her bed. Today, after school, she stopped to buy a bouquet of flowers. Fluted blue flowers that remind her of spring.

How long will it take for her father and Kimberly to notice the changes she's made?

Will they notice?

14

Peggy Sheffield is not the person that Lorelei imagined. Marcus said that she was in her seventies. Marcus said she didn't ride much. So Lorelei pictured someone slow-moving and a little weary. She pictured someone like Mrs. Simmons, the old woman who lives down the street. Mrs. Simmons takes slow, careful steps. She speaks softly.

But Peggy Sheffield's large, hazel eyes twinkle when she talks. And her silver-white hair has been cropped into a bob that makes her look surprisingly young.

"So you're the girl who has taken a fancy to my mare," Mrs. Sheffield — Peggy — says after Marcus introduces them.

"She's incredibly beautiful," Lorelei says.

"I think so, too," Peggy says, and crinkles form at the edges of her eyes. They are intelligent eyes, Lorelei thinks.

Lorelei didn't plan to tell Peggy about her mother. But something about Peggy Sheffield loosens Lorelei's tongue and heart. Soon, her mother's name spills from her lips. Like water.

"Diana Warburton, yes, of course," Peggy says. "I remember your mother."

"You knew her?" Lorelei's eyes widen. "How? When?"

Peggy smiles, and the crinkles around her eyes deepen. "Oh, ages ago. I met you, too. Of course you were so young — four, maybe five. You couldn't possibly remember. It happened right here, at the barn."

Lorelei frowns. "You mean when my mother rode Timothy?"

Peggy nods. "I boarded Artemis's mother here, back then."

Lorelei doesn't have any idea of what to say. Maybe Peggy Sheffield and her mother used to talk to each other. Had her mother ever mentioned Peggy Sheffield? Lorelei will never know.

"I heard about your mother's accident," Peggy says. "I'm terribly sorry."

"Thank you," she says quickly. "I miss her."

The older woman nods kindly. "My mother died when I was sixty-three, and I still miss her. Every day I find something I want to tell her." She shakes her head. "Your mother was far too young. Life can be cruel, unfair."

From somebody else, these words might sound false, like something out of a greeting card.

But from Peggy Sheffield, they feel true.

"Was Artemis's mother white, also?" Lorelei asks after awhile.

"Yes. In fact, the two look so much alike that I sometimes call Artemis by her mother's name."

"What was Artemis's mother's name, then?" Lorelei says.

"Snowflake. My daughter, Sarah, was ten when I bought Artemis's mother. It was Sarah who named her."

No two snowflakes are alike, Lorelei remembers her mother saying.

Peggy studies her closely. "Now then," she says. "Why doesn't Marcus put a saddle on my mare?"

"Really?" Lorelei feels her heart lift.

But then she remembers what day it is and why she's here. She looks from Peggy to Marcus. "I'm afraid I can't today. I have to go back to work."

"I've already spoken to Marion," Peggy says. "She's happy to give you an extra hour today. She's already told me how good you are with the horses."

"It's true," Marcus adds. "Lorelei is a very hard worker. She's also incredibly good with the horses."

"I can see that," Peggy says, and she reaches out and covers Lorelei's hand with her own.

Marcus puts a saddle on Artemis. He cinches the girth beneath her belly. Then he helps Lorelei climb onto her back.

Lorelei is a little uncertain at first. But Artemis stands there patiently.

"She knows her job," Peggy Sheffield says kindly.

"Her job?" Lorelei asks.

"That's right. Before I moved back to Lubbock, she carried Sarah's daughters around. My granddaughters, that is."

Reminded of the mare's gentleness, Lorelei finds this easy to imagine.

"We'll start with a lead rope," Marcus says, "and not a bridle. That way you don't have to think about steering. You just sit tall in the saddle. Really try to feel your seat bones as she walks. Keep your feet light in the stirrups."

"That's a lot to remember," Lorelei says. Seated on Artemis, she feels giddy as if she's high up on a ferris wheel.

"Maybe," he says, "but it's a place to start."

Lorelei and the White Mare

15

"So, how did I do?" Lorelei asks Peggy and Marcus afterward.

"Terrific," Marcus says.

"I agree, but I think you'd benefit from some real lessons," Peggy says, looking directly at Marcus. "And I think that Artemis could benefit from a new friend."

"Absolutely," Marcus agrees, smiling in such a way that Lorelei suspects that the two planned this out beforehand.

"But I can't possibly afford riding lessons," Lorelei says too quickly.

"Maybe not," Peggy says, with that same crinkly smile. "But I can. And Marcus is the perfect teacher."

Marcus bows, blushes. "Thank you, ma'am. From you, that's quite the compliment."

After that, Lorelei's dream about the white mare occurs regularly. She dreams that the mare comes to her in a field of yellow wildflowers. Buttercups, the flowers are called. They were Lorelei's mother's favorites.

One night, she dreams that the white mare grows wings. Lorelei touches the wings in the dream. They are soft, like feathers.

When Lorelei tells Margaret what happened, Margaret says, "It's a sign."

"A sign?" Lorelei frowns. It's Friday in the middle of December, some ten days after Lorelei's first lesson. She and Margaret are sitting in the coffee shop. "I don't get it."

"Come on, Lorelei," Margaret says, rolling her eyes. "This lady lets you ride her horse. Marcus is going to give you lessons. I bet he set it up. You know he's interested in you."

"No, no, he's not," Lorelei says, though she can feel herself blushing.

"Wake up, Lorelei," Margaret says, setting her coffee cup down with a slight clatter. "He took you to just about the fanciest new restaurant in town. He offered to ask Peggy Sheffield to let you ride Artemis. If this isn't a sign of interest, I don't know what is."

"You're just a romantic," Lorelei says, pointing to the love story in Margaret's book bag. Margaret started reading romance novels in fourth grade. She watches old movies like *Endless Love* and *Gone with the Wind*. She quotes lines from love poems.

When Lorelei and Margaret met in the first grade, Margaret already had a boyfriend. His name was Pete, and he collected yo-yos and rubber worms. For Valentine's Day, he gave Margaret a rubber bracelet shaped like a green worm. She loved it and displayed it on her wrist as if it were solid gold.

Now that they're sixteen, Margaret is one of the few people who still sends Valentines. She signs each one in pink ink and draws a little heart around her name. It makes sense, then, that Margaret would be convinced that Marcus is falling in love with Lorelei. And vice versa.

But Lorelei doesn't believe this to be so. Or maybe she is afraid of letting herself believe it. She's gotten used to hiding her feelings. Since her mother died, and especially since her father married Kimberly and became happy again, she's had to.

Even so, once a week, on Thursday afternoons, Lorelei drives over to the stable for her lesson. Marcus is always happy to see her. He always shares a story and brings her a soda or a bottle of juice. They talk about school, the horses, their likes and dislikes. He teaches her how to groom Artemis and saddle her. He helps Lorelei learn the parts of a horse's body.

And on the weekends when she's at work, they often eat lunch together. But he never tries to kiss her. He doesn't even try to hold her hand.

"We're just friends, Margaret," Lorelei tells her again today.

"So you think," Margaret says, twirling a lock of long, blonde hair around her finger. "Just give it time."

Romance or no romance, Lorelei cannot deny that she is happier than she's been in a long time. After saying goodbye to Margaret, she walks down Broadway. She pauses in front of a toy shop window. A plush horse catches her eye. She goes inside and buys it. There are just ten days until Christmas. The plush horse will make a perfect gift.

She walks down Broadway with a spring in her step. She is imagining her next lesson with Artemis. She likes the feel of the mare's broad, supple back. Riding Artemis, Lorelei feels both secure and happy.

At home, Lorelei walks with a lighter step. She laughs more and asks her father and Kimberly about their day. She sets the table sometimes and offers to do the dishes.

One afternoon, she comes home with a bouquet of pink and white lilies.

Their dizzyingly sweet fragrance fills the house.

* * *

Kimberly settles on a color for the nursery. "Mint green," she tells Lorelei. "And we'll hang lacy white curtains on the windows. Maybe you can paint blue stars on the ceiling, Lorelei, and a big, yellow moon."

"Of course," Lorelei says. "I'd be glad to help. I could even do some of the walls. I like that kind of work."

"Wonderful," Kimberly says, exchanging a look with Lorelei's father.

The week before Christmas, Lorelei's winter holiday begins. On Monday morning, she drinks a cup of coffee while taping the edges of the windows and baseboards in preparation for painting.

"Wow," Kimberly says, when she finds her in the nursery. "I knew you wanted to help. But I didn't expect you to do this on your first day off from school."

"The sooner the better, right?" Lorelei says. "I mean, the baby is due at the end of February."

"True," Kimberly says, and smiles. "Let me go get the paint," Kimberly says. "And we can get started together. It would be nice to share a project. We've never done that before."

"Yes, it would," Lorelei says, surprised. And as she speaks these words, she realizes that she means them. Another small swell of happiness rises within her.

Lorelei and the White Mare

16

Every December twenty-fourth, Marion Parsons hosts her annual Christmas Eve Party. It rarely snows in West Texas, but this evening a light snow is falling as Lorelei drives over to the stable. By the time she arrives, the few trees are dusted with a spun-sugar whiteness and the landscape glows.

Lorelei hasn't seen Peggy Sheffield since that Saturday afternoon nearly three weeks ago. Still, she has made Peggy a Christmas gift to show her gratitude. Lorelei looks around for Peggy, but she cannot find her anywhere in the crowd gathered inside the riding arena. Tonight, the guard rails have been decorated with red and white lights. Christmas music plays in the background. The whole atmosphere is incredibly festive.

"Oh, I guess I didn't tell you that she's not coming," Marcus explains when he finds her. He is wearing a thick, black sweater that makes his broad shoulders look even broader.

"Not coming?" Lorelei says.

"Peggy drove back to Albuquerque for the holiday."

"Oh, of course, her daughter's there."

She is aware of the package she has brought for Peggy, carefully layered Christmas cookies between sheets of waxed paper. Earlier this afternoon, she rolled out the lemon-butter dough and cut out shapes: a tree, a reindeer, a partridge, a horse. Oh well, she thinks, the cookies will keep.

"I have something for you," Marcus says, after he brings Lorelei a glass of spiced cider.

"Really? I never expected..." she says, pretending surprise. The truth is she brought him a present, too. Tucked into her backpack, along with a box of buttery sugar cookies, is the red and green flannel shirt that she found at Dillard's.

Marcus goes to his locker, then returns with a big box wrapped in silvery paper and tied with a red velvet ribbon. "For you," he says, placing it in Lorelei's lap.

Carefully, she unwraps the package. Inside she finds a pair of very soft, chocolate-brown leather gloves.

"They're riding gloves, and they're lined with Thinsulate to keep your hands warm during the winter."

"Thank you." She slips them onto her bare hands. "I love them. I have something for you, too."

"Really?" He smiles so brightly that Margaret's suspicions flood Lorelei's mind, and she blushes.

Marcus compliments Lorelei's cookies as soon as he bites into a reindeer.

"There's more," she says, handing him the larger present.

He folds back the tissue paper and looks at the shirt. "Size medium," he says. "How did you know? And red's my favorite color."

Lorelei shrugs. "Lucky guess?"

"It's exactly what I would have chosen for myself," Marcus says. "Thank you."

They sit side by side, and his hand nudges closer to hers. Was Margaret right after all?

"There you are!" Marion Parsons calls out.

Marcus's hand returns to his lap.

Tonight, Marion wears a cranberry turtleneck dress with a gold belt and her riding boots. She stands six feet tall, and her black hair is still as dark as it was when she was Lorelei's age. Marion must be at least fifty-five.

"You look wonderful tonight, Marion," Marcus says.

She smiles. "You, too, and Lorelei," she says, "what a pretty sweater."

Lorelei feels herself blush. The sweater is cotton candy pink. Margaret chose it for her sixteenth birthday.

"Lorelei," Marion continues. "I know it's not your night to work, but is there any way you could help Ricardo out tonight?"

Even though she is wearing the pretty pink sweater and her best jeans, Lorelei stands up right away. "Of course, what do you need?"

"The water in the horses' buckets has frozen," Marion says. "If you could get to work on the buckets in the small barn..."

"Sure, right now," Lorelei says, glancing across the way at Artemis, whose white body glows in the soft light.

"I'll help you," Marcus says.

Lorelei shakes her head. "No," she says. "This won't take long. Besides, it looks like your fans are waiting to talk to you."

Sure enough, six of Marcus's students are approaching.

They are all girls between the ages of eleven and fourteen. They wear their long hair in braids or a loose ponytail. Each one is carrying a present. For Marcus.

Outside, the chill air penetrates Lorelei's wool coat. There's a slight wind tonight, and the snow is accumulating quickly now.

As Lorelei makes her way over to the small barn, she catches sight of Toby and Ida Red, two of the horses who live outside. It seems that Ricardo forgot to put their blankets on. They whinny as Lorelei passes. She calls to them, then reminds herself to ask Marion about their blankets when she finishes in the small barn.

Soon, she hears footsteps behind her. She remembers the feel of Marcus's hand nearing her own, the electricity between them. Or did she only imagine it?

But when she turns around, it's Woody, the border collie. He bounds over to her, wagging his tail. "Good to see you, friend," she says, though her pockets are empty of treats tonight.

The small barn's doors have been closed, sealing the heat inside. She grabs a steel pick from the feed closet, then approaches Noah's stall.

The old horse nickers, and she produces a peppermint from her coat pocket. She will give every horse in the barn a peppermint tonight.

She gets to work breaking up the ice in his bucket. Afterward, she tops it off with water. In another hour, the surface will freeze over. But for now, at least, he can drink.

It takes Lorelei more than half an hour to finish up in the small barn. In the last stall, she finds Copper Penny and her mother.

She remembers what Marion said about weaning Copper Penny before Christmas. The process hasn't begun yet because Marion has been too busy. And Lorelei is glad. She gives the filly and her mother two peppermints each.

"Merry Christmas," she tells them.

On the way back, Lorelei runs into Ricardo, whose face is almost completely hidden by a thick wool scarf.

"Ida Red and Toby..." she begins.

"I know," he says. "I forgot their blankets. I'll fetch them now."

Back inside the big barn, the air is deliciously warm, and the Christmas Eve Party is in full swing. Many guests have paired off for dancing. Marcus is among them. His partner is Sasha, the pretty riding teacher who is also a senior at the university.

Lorelei thinks about the lovely riding gloves that Marcus gave her. She tries not to feel jealous.

Several of the horses' owners stop Lorelei to wish her a Merry Christmas and give her a gift. "We're so grateful for all you do," several tell her. "I always know that I can count on you to make sure my Buddy is alright," another says.

And from shy Elise Winter, a former librarian: "You're a treasure, my dear, a real treasure." Accepting her gift from Elise, Lorelei is sure that it's a book.

At ten o'clock, the party begins to break up. Several of the guests plan to go to Midnight Mass.

The last time Lorelei went to Midnight Mass, she was fourteen. She sat between her parents and sang "Away in a Manger" and "Silent Night." The candles on the altar shone like liquid gold.

After the service, they stood before the nativity scene and studied it. Lorelei loved the delicacy of the hand-carved figurines. The creche itself had been carved from wood. Real moss lined the ground. Lorelei's mother promised that they would make a miniature version. Somehow, they never found the time.

Without even thinking about it, Lorelei finds herself drifting across the arena to the far end of the barn. Soon, she is sliding open the door to the white mare's stall. Then she is standing beside the horse and burying her nose in Artemis's white mane. The white mare remains very still, and her large body exudes calming warmth. She smells of hay and oats and winter.

Lorelei is seized by the desire to curl up in the stall and go to sleep here. After all, the straw on the floor is clean. There is plenty of room. It's a crazy idea, she knows, totally ridiculous. She will have to go home soon.

"Merry Christmas," she tells Artemis, and she retrieves a handful of peppermints from her pocket. This time, however, Lorelei sucks on a peppermint too.

Eventually, Lorelei realizes that someone is watching her. When the door opens, it is Marcus who steps inside the stall. His cheeks are flushed, and his blue eyes are shining. "I've been looking for you," he says. "Something told me I'd find you here."

Is it Marcus who kisses Lorelei? Or is it Lorelei who kisses him? All she knows is that their lips find each other. The kiss is warm and tastes like peppermint.

Lorelei leans into Marcus, breathes in his musky scent. He is comfortable, warm. They stand together in the stall for a long time, the white mare beside them.

Soon, someone — Marion or Ricardo — begins switching off the lights. In a few moments, the barn will be cloaked in darkness.

"I guess we'd better go," Marcus says, standing very close to her.

"Just a minute." Lorelei wraps her arms around the white mare's neck. She presses her cheek to the long muscle that begins at Artemis's ear and ends at her shoulder.

Then she takes Marcus's hand and lets him lead her through the shadowy barn. Through the open doorway, she can see that the night is clearing. Driving home, she might even see the moon and stars.

17

Lorelei's lessons go well. She finds her balance in the saddle and keeps her toes up and her heels down, as Marcus instructed. And she manages to keep from tugging on the reins.

"You sure you haven't ridden before?" Marcus sometimes teases.

"Cross my heart," Lorelei replies.

It's the end of January, and she can now trot around the arena on her own. Artemis has a steady gait, and she is careful with Lorelei. Some of the horses tend to speed off or "run away" with their riders, especially the beginners.

But Artemis never goes too fast. The white mare's kindness reminds Lorelei of what Peggy said when they first met: "Artemis knows her job."

Sometimes, Marcus sets up cones in the arena and has Lorelei practice steering around them. "This is a lot harder than I thought," she says, laughing. "And it sure is harder than it looks."

"Imagine you're riding Artemis through a corridor," he says. "Build a wall on either side of you. Tell yourself that you have to move her through the passageway without knocking into the wall."

"Okay," Lorelei says. She imagines a stone wall like the one she saw on the coast off the Atlantic Ocean years ago. She takes care not to get too close to the wall. Her steering improves.

"Good job," Marcus calls out.

After riding, Lorelei lingers at the barn to groom Artemis. She begins with the curry comb, then moves on to the soft brush. She especially enjoys brushing

Artemis's silky nose and long, muscular neck. She brushes her mane and tail until they shimmer silver-white.

Marcus shows her how to massage Artemis's neck by tracing the long muscle that begins at her ear and ends at her shoulder. "Use the palm of your hand," he says. "Apply a little pressure and be sure to do the massage on both sides."

Artemis nickers with pleasure.

One day he rubs the gum line of Artemis's mouth with his fingertips.

"That's a little weird, wouldn't you say?" Lorelei asks.

"Nope," Marcus replies. "This actually relaxes her back. Here," he points to Artemis's mouth, "you give it a try."

And she does and finds herself amazed that Artemis actually likes it.

In addition to coming for her lessons, Lorelei begins showing up often to watch Marcus ride his handsome bay warmblood, Dakota. Bay is very close to black, and Dakota is a sleek, muscular creature. He is also the kind of horse to "run away" with an inexperienced rider. But he's friendly and gentle on the ground. And he loves peppermints.

"So do I," Marcus says, after one of his rides.

But it's not the candy he wants. It's a kiss from Lorelei, whose breath smells like peppermint.

When the weather's good, Peggy Sheffield likes to stop by the barn. She seems a little more tired than she did before the holidays, but she's always cheerful.

She praised Lorelei's Christmas cookies so much that Lorelei continues to bring her snickerdoodles, sugar cookies, and pinwheels.

"I'll lose my figure if I'm not careful," Peggy teases when Lorelei hands over a package of butterscotch brownies.

Now, in addition to spending Saturday and Sunday at the barn, Lorelei is there during the week, too. She has her riding lesson on Thursday, and she tries to practice on Tuesdays as well.

On the days that Lorelei cannot come to the barn, she finds herself missing Artemis. Lorelei misses her smell, her warmth, the light in her dark eyes.

Lorelei believes that Artemis misses her, too. How does Lorelei know this? No one says anything to her. She simply senses it. She can feel Artemis thinking about her. Lorelei knows this sounds strange, but she cannot deny it.

"I don't think it's strange at all," Marcus says when she tells him how she feels. "Horses are paranormal."

"Para-what?" Lorelei asks. They are sitting together outside the barn. It snowed again two days ago, but today the sun is out and the landscape glistens.

"It means they can sense things that we can't."

"You've lost me."

He laughs. "Let me give you an example. In the wild, horses live in a herd. If one of them gets lost, that lost horse will try to let the others know where he is."

"By whinnying?" Lorelei asks.

"Yeah, sure, but if the horse is too far away, he uses his mind or his energy or whatever you want to call it to get in touch with the others."

"Oh, I think I get it," Lorelei says.

She is reminded of her dreams about the white mare. She still has them, and often there are two white mares in her vision. Little by little, she's realizing that these dreams are helping her to cope with her grief over her mother. And even though Lorelei still misses her mother deeply, the hollowed out feeling is less intense.

If grief is a box, then Lorelei can carry her load more easily now.

She doesn't tell Marcus or Margaret about her dreams. As for telling Artemis, there's no need. There's a current of energy between them. Feelings of peace and contentment wash over Lorelei when she's with the white mare.

It's not just at the barn where changes are happening. They're happening at home, too. Yes, Lorelei still feels separate from her father and Kimberly. But the distance between them is diminishing.

Not that Lorelei's told either one of them how much the world of the stable is impacting her. Sure, her father and Kimberly see her muddy riding boots in the hall, and they've noticed the breeches she now wears to ride.

But they don't know about Artemis or Peggy Sheffield. Marcus, they have met. He often comes over to go for a walk with Lorelei. Or he picks her up for a movie, dinner, and sometimes for ice cream at the old fifties diner on Buddy Holly Avenue.

"I like Marcus just fine," Lorelei's father says, one especially cold evening at the end of January. "But I think he's a little old for you, Lorelei. How old is he, anyway? Twenty-one?"

"Twenty-two," Lorelei says, glancing out at the wintry landscape.

Her father frowns. "What about the guys your own age? Jeremy, for example? He was always so responsible, and he's president of the debate team — a really good sign. What happened to him?"

"We drifted apart," Lorelei says quietly.

Jeremy had been her last boyfriend. They saw each other for six months, and yes, there was no doubt they were happy.

Until Lorelei's mother died.

"Well, that's too bad," her father says now.

Lorelei knows the real reason her father doesn't approve of Marcus. It's the fact that he didn't finish college. And her father, a history professor, believes in Education with a capital E. To Lorelei's surprise, it is Kimberly who comes to Marcus's defense.

"He's a good guy, James," Kimberly says later. "You should be happy. Lorelei's happier now. And just think about the beautiful job she did in the nursery. The ceiling is like a dream landscape — the moon and stars. Really, babe, this Marcus is a good development. He comes into the bakery sometimes. He's always polite, friendly. I like him."

Lorelei is in the other room at the time, and she has no context — no clues — to the conversation. Yet she's amazed. It's not just that Kimberly is defending Marcus. What amazes Lorelei is that Kimberly actually noticed her sadness.

Is it possible, Lorelei asks herself now, that she hasn't been seeing Kimberly clearly because of her own grief? The possibility that this is so lifts a further weight from Lorelei's shoulders. The box gets a little bit lighter.

Of course, Kimberly only has part of the picture. Kimberly believes that Marcus is the sole reason that grief has loosed hold on Lorelei's heart.

What Kimberly doesn't know is how essential the white mare, Artemis, has become. The white mare is fundamental. She is like breath, like fresh air and water.

Lorelei and the White Mare

18

To celebrate all the progress that Lorelei is making riding and connecting with Artemis, Peggy invites her over to dinner. Whereas Lorelei lives just outside the city limits, Peggy's house sits on one of those rare tree-lined streets near the university. Her two story house is unusual for Lubbock. It has a real, shingle roof and reminds Lorelei of the houses she saw on a trip to New England.

"Welcome," Peggy says, ushering her inside.

The rooms are large and cozy, with comfortable, old-fashioned furniture and plenty of art on the walls. Knick-knacks fill the cupboards. In the sitting room, there's a woven rug on the floor. Two tabby cats nest in baskets near the window. A third is curled up in an armchair by the fireplace. It is the kind of house that Lorelei would like for herself one day.

Peggy looks lovely in a peach floral dress. The odd thing is that the dress seems a little too big, and Lorelei wonders if Peggy has lost weight.

She holds out a box of cookies.

"You spoil me, my dear," Peggy says, and laughs.

Lorelei has grown comfortable with Peggy, but this evening she is just a bit nervous. Lorelei has never been alone with her before. She isn't quite sure what they will talk about.

"Why don't we sit and have a cup of tea before dinner?" Peggy says.

Lorelei warms to the idea. She loves tea and has even convinced Marcus to start drinking it. Usually, he, like Margaret, prefers coffee.

As the sun sets beyond the windows, they talk about the stable. After a while, Peggy journeys further back in time to talk about Artemis's beginnings. "Such a funny little filly she was," Peggy says. "She was born in March during an unexpected snowstorm, and she was so tiny that I was afraid she might not make it."

Thinking about Artemis's sturdy build, Lorelei finds a tiny Artemis hard to imagine.

"Just to be safe," Peggy says, "I spent the first four nights sleeping in the stable with Artemis and her mother. I brought out extra quilts, and I even set up the space heater. It was a little rocky at first. She didn't gain enough weight during the first ten days, and again I was afraid. But then," Peggy says, fixing her hazel eyes on Lorelei, "it was as if the little filly decided that she wanted to stay for a while."

"Wanted to stay?" Lorelei leans forward, curious.

"That's right. I had this strange feeling that Artemis made a choice. She began to nurse more frequently, and she became more inquisitive. By the time the snow melted and the crocuses came out, she was thriving."

Lorelei sits silently for a while. One of the cats, the calico named Jessie, jumps into her lap.

"I had reason to be afraid, you see," Peggy says. "Before Artemis, there was another foal — and that one didn't make it."

"That must have been terrible," Lorelei says. She is thinking about Copper Penny, the lively little filly.

"It was," Peggy says. "Both my daughter and I cried for weeks after that first foal died. Fortunately, Artemis did really well."

"How old is Artemis?" Lorelei asks now.

"Eleven," Peggy says, "and if she's anything like her mom, she'll live for another twenty years."

"I hope so," Lorelei says, stroking the cat.

"Thing is, I won't live that long," Peggy says, her voice growing serious.

"I bet you will," Lorelei says. But when she looks up at Peggy, the older woman's face matches her tone.

"No, Lorelei, I won't."

It is not long before Peggy mentions that fearful word "cancer" and "nine months, maybe a year at the most."

"I can't believe that," Lorelei says, and it feels as if the floor is dropping out from underneath her. Or maybe it's her stomach. The room begins to spin.

"I have a hard time believing it, myself," Peggy says. "I started chemotherapy last month. That's part of the reason I moved back to Lubbock. I know one of the oncologists at the medical center. She's one of the best in her field."

Lorelei's mind swims with questions, but before she can say anything more, Peggy stands up.

"Oh dear, I hadn't planned to get all gloomy tonight. It's just that I trust you so with Artemis. You're so good with her. And she, well, she is a little bit like a second daughter. But I've said enough for now, perhaps too much. Let's go and eat. I fixed a casserole for supper and some parsnips. You do like vegetables, don't you?"

"Yes," Lorelei says, still shaken, "of course."

During dinner, and later over more tea and dessert served in a smaller room, Peggy tells Lorelei about her daughter Sarah and her granddaughters. She tells her about the places she's visited: Italy, the Swiss

Alps, Morocco when it was still safe for an American to travel there.

Lorelei is interested, and she listens closely. Even so, she cannot forget about what Peggy has said. She has cancer. Within the year, she will die. How can this be possible?

"I'm sorry, I see that I've upset you," Peggy says, rearranging one of the white snowdrops in a crystal vase. "Tonight was — it is — supposed to be a celebration."

"No," Lorelei says, "don't say that. You're upset, and you needed to talk about it."

"Yes, you're right. To be honest, I'm angry," Peggy tells her now. "I'm seventy-four years old. My mother lived to be ninety. I thought I was entitled to at least another fifteen years."

Lorelei stirs more sugar into her tea, though she usually drinks it black. "Maybe you'll beat it," she says.

"I wish I could, and I don't plan to go down without a fight. No one else at the barn knows, not even Marion," Peggy says. "As I said, part of the reason I told you, Lorelei, is because I know how much you care about

Artemis. And," she pauses, "I know how much Artemis cares about you."

"I do care about her, enormously. What's going to happen to her?" Lorelei says.

"Well, I'm not sure. My daughter, Sarah, is very willing to keep her. She lives on a ranch outside of Albuquerque. She already has three horses. It wouldn't be difficult for Artemis to settle in there."

Lorelei feels a chill wash over her. Is it possible that she will lose Artemis just as she's getting to know her?

Not that Artemis was ever mine to lose, Lorelei tells herself. Yet she doesn't quite believe this. There's that connection between them. Lorelei feels it in her soft tissue. She feels it in her bones.

"My dear," Peggy says, laying a hand on Lorelei's own. "Please, don't look so grim. I suppose I haven't been entirely honest with you or with myself. The other reason I asked you hear tonight is to gauge your interest in looking after her."

Lorelei's heartbeat quickens. "What do you mean?" she asks, hearing the eagerness in her voice.

"Well, I haven't thought it all the way through, at least not yet. But I suppose I'm suggesting that Artemis stay here at the stable. If it works out, perhaps you could keep her."

Lorelei's heart is pounding. "Are you serious?"

"I would need to discuss it with Sarah, of course," Peggy says. "My granddaughters love Artemis, too, but they have other horses, other interests. Artemis needs someone who would be devoted to her."

* * *

Lorelei spends the next few days in a daze. She is deeply troubled by Peggy's cancer. Having come to care for Peggy, Lorelei cannot imagine losing her. But there is another side to her sorrow this time. The beautiful, mysterious white mare might actually come to belong to Lorelei.

On the days when Peggy stops by the stable, she laughs and talks with Marion and the other teachers and riders. She lingers with Artemis. Except for the fact that she has grown thinner, no one would ever guess that she was ill.

One bright afternoon, she even saddles the white mare up and rides around the arena. Peggy sits tall in the saddle. She looks grounded. Together, she and Artemis move like velvet.

* * *

A few days before Valentine's Day, Lorelei is walking Artemis outside on a lead rope. She likes to walk beside her along the long fence line. When Artemis pauses to sniff the ground or when her ears perk up at a sudden noise in the distance, Lorelei follows her movements closely.

Peggy is supposed to come to the stable that day to watch Lorelei's lesson, and Lorelei is on the lookout for her blue Subaru.

She is going to learn to canter today, and she's both excited and nervous. A horse's canter is comparable to a human being's jog, Marcus has said. It's quicker than the trot but also more fluid, less bumpy.

A few minutes before her lesson, Marcus comes outside. His brow is furrowed, and he looks worried.

"What is it?" Lorelei asks. "What's wrong?"

"It's Peggy Sheffield," he says.

Marcus goes on to tell Lorelei that they've taken Peggy to the hospital. And soon Lorelei hears herself tell Marcus what Peggy confided to her. She tells him about the cancer and the prognosis.

When Marcus begins to cry, Lorelei enfolds him in her arms and holds on tight. He cares about Peggy, too. And she's not the only one who's lost someone. Marcus's mother died when he was four. Like Peggy, she died of cancer.

Beside them, Artemis remains very still. So still, in fact, that Lorelei believes the white mare knows that something is wrong. Paranormal, Marcus calls horses. Meaning: they can sense things — pick up on things — because they are so sensitive to the energy around them.

Yes, Lorelei thinks, as Artemis nuzzles her cheek, the white mare knows that Peggy is ill.

19

Peggy comes home from the hospital a few days later. "The tumors are more aggressive than my doctor thought," she tells Lorelei. "I'll be lucky if I make it through the summer."

Peggy doesn't cry, but she looks old, and very tired. The sparkle has gone out of Peggy's eyes. And the crinkles that form at the edges of her eyes and mouth when she smiles? They, too, are different somehow.

"Because Peggy didn't smile," Lorelei will tell Marcus later.

*　*　*

Kimberly goes into labor ten days after Valentine's Day. Lorelei is at the stable mucking out stalls when her father calls.

"It's early yet," he says, excitement pulsing at the edges of his voice. "But if you can make it over to the hospital after you finish up, that would be fantastic."

"Yes, of course," Lorelei says. She is in the small barn in Lady's stall, and she finds this fitting somehow. After all, Lady gave birth to two foals in this very spot.

Right now, Lorelei misses her mother intensely. "Mom," she whispers into the chilly, February air. "Mom..." Her voice trails off.

Except for her and Woody, the ever-loyal Border Collie, the barn is empty. Beyond the barn, the landscape is wintry, for it has snowed again.

In a few hours, I will have a half-brother or half-sister, Lorelei tells herself. She's known this for months, of course, but it's only now that it hits her so hard and she has to sit down. It's there on the stall floor that Marcus finds her. How much time has passed, she cannot possibly say.

"Marion's been looking for you," he says. "Are you okay?"

"Kimberly's in labor," she says. "Everything's going to change again."

He kneels beside her. "Change is the only thing that we can count on."

Lorelei wraps her arms around his neck, buries her face against him.

"Pretty wise words," she whispers.

"Come on," he says, after a while. "Why don't I finish up in here and you head on over to the hospital to be with your dad?"

"But I have so much to do still, and you have lessons this afternoon."

"Really," he says. "You should go and be with your father. Besides, you'll need to take the roads slow given the weather. Really, go," he says again. "Trust me."

"All right," Lorelei says. "Thank you."

On her way out, she makes her way over to the paddock where Artemis spends her days with two other mares, one of whom is Lady.

The white mare comes over to her right away. Lorelei presses her cheek to the horse's nose, breathes in her rich scent. "My stepmother's having a baby," she whispers. "I'll be back soon."

Not until she's on the road north does Lorelei realize that this is the first time that she's called Kimberly 'my stepmother.'

* * *

Fourteen hours after Kimberly's labor pains began, she gives birth to an eight-and-a-half-pound baby boy.

"Wake up, sweetie," her father says to Lorelei. "I want you to meet someone."

His voice seeps into her dreams — it's been so long since he called her 'sweetie.' She opens her eyes to meet the tiniest person she has ever seen. He has a fuzzy cap of dark hair, and his eyes are the blue of midnight.

"May I hold him?" Lorelei asks.

"Of course."

The next thing she knows, he is in her arms.

"Hello there," she says softly.

"We're going to call him Nathaniel," her father says.

"Really?" Lorelei keeps her eyes on the tiny newborn in her arms.

Nathaniel is the boy's name that she loves most in the world.

* * *

Despite the cold winter, spring comes early that year. By mid-March, the afternoon air is sun-warmed. The daffodils bloom, followed by the tulips. Tight, green buds dot the branches of the trees.

The horses begin shedding their winter coats. When Lorelei brushes Artemis, it's not unusual for a shoebox-sized pile of fur to accumulate at her feet.

Peggy Sheffield's condition doesn't improve, but it does seem to stabilize. She is a third of the way through the chemotherapy. She has one week of treatment, then one week off. The treatment weeks are the rugged ones, and she keeps to her bed. Afternoons or evenings, Lorelei often stops by with books, tea, flowers.

"I picked these at the stable," Lorelei says, coming over one bright Thursday. She presents Peggy with a bouquet of tiny, white wildflowers.

"Oh, how beautiful," Peggy says. "And lemon cake, you brought me that, too."

Lorelei cuts two slices and places each on a china plate. Lemon is one of the few flavors that curbs Peggy's nausea. They fix tea. Afterwards, they sit for a while and talk, the cats nestled around them.

Since their conversation in February, Peggy has said nothing to Lorelei about what will happen to Artemis.

And Lorelei, in turn, has said nothing to Marcus or to anyone else about the possibility that she might keep her. Sometimes, she even wonders if she dreamed that conversation with Peggy.

Meanwhile, baby Nathaniel is thriving. Watching him, Lorelei sometimes thinks about what Peggy said about Artemis's decision to stay after she was born.

Nathaniel loves to lie in his crib and gaze up at the ceiling with its moon and stars. He gurgles and coos and is reaching for his toes.

After the first three weeks, Kimberly goes back to working half days at the bakery. She may be a new mother, but she also has a business to run. Kimberly always comes home tired and eager to be with Nathaniel.

To help, Lorelei cooks dinner pretty regularly. Often her father helps her. Side by side, they will stand chopping vegetables for a stew or a stir fry.

"We can leave out the chicken tonight," her father says one evening.

She looks at him, grateful and surprised.

"I appreciate all that you're doing around here," he tells her then.

"I'm trying," she says.

"I know."

He pulls her close, and she relaxes against him, reminded of the years of hugs, a lifetime of hugs. When she was little and would fall and scrape a knee or an elbow, it was her father she'd often run to. And how many nights had he comforted her when she'd had a bad dream?

Yet tonight is the first time, in longer than Lorelei can remember, when her father has reached out to her like this.

And she is grateful. She leans into him, hugs him back.

20

Lorelei turns seventeen on the first day of April. To celebrate, Marcus borrows one of Marion's trailers. He loads his own horse, Dakota, then Artemis.

"Where are we going?" she asks him just before they set out that morning. It's a Wednesday, and she's skipping school.

"I told you, it's a surprise," he says, then kisses her on the nose.

"And Peggy said it was okay? To take Artemis out in a trailer, I mean?"

"Yes, of course," Marcus says.

Eagerly, she climbs into the passenger side of the truck, and then the two of them make their way onto the county road that funnels off into Clovis Highway. For breakfast, they share a thermos of coffee and a tin of Lorelei's gingerbread. They have fresh strawberries, too.

An hour and a half into the drive, Lorelei sees the first signs of Caprock Canyon, and then she knows where they're going. To the state park. To ride.

"Everyone thinks West Texas is flat," she hears herself tell Marcus. "But when you see this landscape, you realize what it means to live on the high plains."

By "this landscape," Lorelei is referring to the way the level ground gives way to the reddish-pink walls of the canyon.

With the exception of riding Artemis on the small patch of land adjacent to the stable, Lorelei has only ridden in the arena.

Setting out on this turquoise-blue-sky day, the canyon opens up before them. And Lorelei feels her body and her spirit expand.

Artemis appreciates the change, too. As soon as they find the trail, she pricks up her ears and looks around. She is curious and interested.

"I never thought riding could be like this," Lorelei says, as the spring breeze rustles her hair and sweeps against her skin.

"It's pretty gorgeous out here, isn't it?" Marcus says.

They ride for a good two hours, moving at a slow but steady pace, deeper and deeper into the canyon. Towards noon, they arrive at a stream surrounded by gnarled mesquite trees, yucca, cacti, and other drought-resistant plants.

"How about some lunch, birthday girl?" Marcus asks.

"Absolutely," Lorelei replies. "I'm starved."

Lorelei leads Artemis over to the stream so that she can drink. The white mare places her front legs in the water and bats it back and forth. She is playing, and Lorelei begins to laugh.

"I wish Peggy could see this," she says.

"Yes," Marcus agrees. "She would be pleased."

Beside them, Dakota just laps at the water.

Marcus has filled a saddlebag with hay, and after they drink, he gives each horse a hearty portion.

"What's for lunch?" Lorelei asks.

"You'll see."

Usually, she fixes the meal. This time Marcus had insisted that he make it.

He spreads a blanket on the sandy soil, and they sit down to cream cheese sandwiches with wafer-thin slices of cucumber. There is a salad of tomatoes, too, and for dessert, a bar of rich, dark chocolate and more strawberries carefully packed in ice.

"I'm impressed," Lorelei says, for Marcus's sandwiches usually consist of peanut butter or some lunch meat.

"Peggy's suggestion," he says.

Lorelei nods. She bites her lip, determined not to cry.

Marcus slips his arm around her. In the past week, Peggy's strength has deteriorated. She is thin, pale, drained.

Even though she doesn't start chemotherapy again until Monday, she has spent most of this week in bed. Lorelei knows that it will be a miracle if she lives through the summer.

Lorelei closes her eyes. She thinks about the first time Peggy came out to the barn. She recalls the sparkle in her hazel eyes, the crinkled beauty of her smile. Such hope Peggy has given her, such happiness.

Peggy's prognosis hasn't changed. The cancer is incurable. The best the doctors can do is buy her a little more time.

"Hey," Marcus says. "I didn't bring a cake, but you still need to make a wish." He cups a candle in his hand and lights it. "Now then," he says, "go ahead."

Lorelei smiles, grateful. She knows what she must wish for. She closes her eyes, breathes deeply, and thinks the words. And when she opens her eyes, it is Artemis whose gaze she meets.

"I hope it comes true," Marcus says, then kisses her deeply.

They stay there together for a long time and hold each other. Beside them, the horses munch contentedly. The breeze is sweet and warm. It is a beautiful day.

"I love you, birthday girl," Marcus says.

"Me, too," Lorelei says, for no one other than her parents — and Margaret — has said such a thing to her before. "I mean, I love you, too."

They both laugh.

* * *

The wish did come true. At least part of it, Lorelei realizes, but only much later.

The exhaustion that Peggy experiences in April gives way to something more hopeful by May. Not that Peggy ever recovers the energy she once had.

But she does come out to the barn again. And on a particularly lovely day in the middle of May, Lorelei helps Peggy saddle up Artemis. (The saddle is now too heavy for Peggy to lift on her own.)

At first, Lorelei thinks Peggy will ride the white mare around the arena.

"I can't stay inside on this beautiful day," Peggy says softly. The familiar, friendly crinkles appear at the edges of her smiling eyes.

Peggy steers Artemis out into the sunlight. April rain has turned the land green, and dark pink henbit blooms in the grass.

Lorelei watches her friend ride. She has begun to think about her own focus in the saddle. "How do you know you're focused?" Marcus asked her just the other day.

At the time, she didn't quite know how to answer.

Here, now, Lorelei understands what he meant. Peggy's chin is tucked and she gazes down, just slightly, so that Lorelei knows she is looking between the white mare's ears.

The only truth in life is change, Marcus said again the other day.

Lorelei knows this to be true. Her brother, Nathaniel, is the biggest proof of that. He's already outgrown two sizes of clothes since he was born.

Yes, everything is changing. She will lose Peggy, as she lost her mother. Lorelei knows this. She's struggling to accept it.

Still, standing there in the May sunlight, Lorelei tries to create a lasting picture of what she sees before her now. And what she sees is a woman and a horse riding together in complete harmony. Right now, the sky is so blue and wide it seems to go on forever. Surely, Lorelei thinks, there must be some things that last.

"Lorelei," Peggy calls. "Lorelei."

Lorelei walks towards her, the warm breeze tickling her skin and tousling her hair. "Yes?" Lorelei calls back. "Do you need anything?"

"There's something I've been meaning to tell you," Peggy says.

Perhaps it's the familiar sparkle that returns to Peggy's eyes just then.

Whatever it is, Lorelei knows what her friend is about to say.

"It's about Artemis," Peggy says. "She needs to stay with you."

Lorelei feels herself grow lighter. She wants to cry out with joy. "Oh, Peggy," is all she can say.

"You belong together. Always remember, it's an extraordinary gift and a blessing when you find someone to love."

Yes, oh yes, Lorelei thinks, as she looks at Peggy and then at Artemis.

A blessing is exactly the right phrase. It is love that lasts.

Lorelei's mother is no longer on this earth. Yet the love remains. As the love will remain for Peggy once she is gone.

"Now, then," Peggy says. "I'm tired. Why don't you take a turn? After all, it is such an exquisite day, the most perfect day of the year."

"Yes," Lorelei says. "It is perfect, this day." Artemis, as if understanding, whinnies in reply.

In memory of Margaret "Peggy" Sheffield Lutherer

About The Author

Jacqueline Kolosov is a poet and prose writer. She has published several novels for teens including *The Red Queen's Daughter* (Hyperion) and *Paris, Modigliani & Me* (Luminis). Along with writing and the visual arts (Modigliani was a contemporary of Picasso), Jacqueline is passionate about horses and knows, first-hand, their strengths as teachers, healers, and beings who enable self-knowledge and growth. Whenever she can, she spends time with her horses and her daughter, Sophia. Together with her family and a menagerie of animals that includes not only horses but dogs, cats, and a white rabbit, Jacqueline currently makes her home in the windswept landscape that is also Lorelei's. She is Professor of English and Director of Creative Writing at

Texas Tech, and you can find out more about her at www.english.ttu.edu. She welcomes emails at jacqueline.kolosov@ttu.edu.

About The Publisher

Story Shares is a nonprofit focused on supporting the millions of teens and adults who struggle with reading by creating a new shelf in the library specifically for them. The ever-growing collection features content that is compelling and culturally relevant for teens and adults, yet still readable at a range of lower reading levels.

Story Shares generates content by engaging deeply with writers, bringing together a community to create this new kind of book. With more intriguing and approachable stories to choose from, the teens and adults who have fallen behind are improving their skills and beginning to discover the joy of reading. For more information, visit storyshares.org.

Easy to Read. Hard to Put Down.

Made in the USA
Middletown, DE
20 January 2023

22671299R00087